Acting Edition

Jennifer Who Is Leaving

by Morgan Gould

SAMUEL FRENCH

No one shall make any changes in this title(s) for the purpose of production. No part of this book may be reproduced, stored in a retrieval system, scanned, uploaded, or transmitted in any form, by any means, now known or yet to be invented, including mechanical, electronic, digital, photocopying, recording, videotaping, or otherwise, without the prior written permission of the publisher. No one shall share this title(s), or any part of this title(s), through any social media or file hosting websites.

For all inquiries regarding motion picture, television, online/digital and other media rights, please contact Concord Theatricals Corp.

MUSIC AND THIRD-PARTY MATERIALS USE NOTE

Licensees are solely responsible for obtaining formal written permission from copyright owners to use copyrighted music and/or other copyrighted third-party materials (e.g. artworks, logos) in the performance of this play and are strongly cautioned to do so. If no such permission is obtained by the licensee, then the licensee must use only original music and materials that the licensee owns and controls. Licensees are solely responsible and liable for clearances of all third-party copyrighted materials, including without limitation music, and shall indemnify the copyright owners of the play(s) and their licensing agent, Concord Theatricals Corp., against any costs, expenses, losses and liabilities arising from the use of such copyrighted third-party materials by licensees. For music, please contact the appropriate music licensing authority in your territory for the rights to any incidental music.

IMPORTANT BILLING AND CREDIT REQUIREMENTS

If you have obtained performance rights to this title, please refer to your licensing agreement for important billing and credit requirements.

JENNIFER WHO IS LEAVING had its world premiere in 2023 at Round House Theater (Ryan Rilette, Artistic Director; Ed Zakreski, Managing Director; and Naysan Mojgani, Associate Artistic Director/Festival Producer) in Bethesda, Maryland. The performance was directed by Morgan Gould, with dramaturgy by Lauren Halvorsen, sets by Paige Hathaway, costumes by Ivania Stack, lighting design by Emma Deane, sound design by Justin Schmitz, and props design by Dre Moore. The Production Stage Manager was Rachael Albert and the Assistant Stage Manager was Ilana Simon. Shana Laski was the Assistant Director. The cast was as follows:

NAN . . . . Nancy Robinette

JENNIFER . . . . Kimberly Gilbert

LILI . . . . Annie Fang

JOEY . . . . .Floyd King

CHARACTERS

NAN – Late 60s–70s, white, senior employee at the Dunkin Donuts-like Donut Chain, thick Massachusetts (Southie, perhaps) accent.

JENNIFER – Mid to late 40s, white, a nurse's aide, very tired, also has a Massachusetts accent.

LILI – Late teens, a high school student and part-time employee at the store, she can be AAPI or Latine. No accent.

JOEY – 80s, white, a patient of Jennifer's who is prone to outbursts, he's gay and a mean old queen [though it doesn't matter if the audience knows that part], who loves to be an asshole – like he TRULY enjoys it. Funny until he is not. No accent for him, either.

Never appears, but in case you want to know...

CHUCK – 60s, Nan's husband, wears Boston sports paraphernalia, also has a thick accent and a bad knee.

SETTING

At the Dunkin Donuts-like chain just off Route 495 in Wareham, MA. It's not shabby. It's overly new and corporate-looking. It's the last stop before "the bridge."

TIME

Late Winter. Late Night.

AUTHOR'S NOTES

Please make best efforts to engage a disability consultant or someone who can help you responsibly stage Joey as a wheelchair user – especially given the complexities and layers of caretaker abuse and WPV (workplace violence) against nurses.

If you do not cast Jennifer and/or Nan as AT LEAST NORMAL SIZED or plus-size or fat actresses, I do not believe you fundamentally understand this play or these people. No one who works at a donut shop on a HIGHWAY and is over the age of forty is PERFECTLY THIN, my god, use your head.

When Joey sings, it's more like sing-song annoying teasing. Not "singing."

Nan's phone calls should be snappy and fun, but take enough time that we should feel Chuck's presence and intuitively know what he is saying (which only works if Nan knows what he is saying and takes the time to hear him).

Lili's final monologue is VERY tricky. It shouldn't feel mean or punishing, but its rhythm should build slightly so by the end it feels relentless and we watch the initial welcoming kindness drain out of the actress as she speaks it. The goal is for the audience to first be like "why is this in the show" but then by the end the amassed list – spoken with barely any breaths in between – makes the audience see that reliance on women's invisible labor transcends socioeconomics and generation.

(A cheesy song like Christina Aguilera's "Genie In A Bottle" flares up as the house lights come down and everything blacks out. Soon, the song fades, tinnily coming from shitty speakers onstage as the lights come up on a Dunkin Donuts-like donut shop/chain. The song is playing as part of the cheery pop mix we will hear throughout the show.)*

*(**NAN**, wearing the store uniform, leans on the counter, a huge, long phone cord tethering her behind the counter. She has a lanyard representing a popular New England football team with a bajillion keys on it.** She speaks loudly into the phone. She's not yelling, exactly, she's just speaking in the way all women with thick Massachusetts accents speak...as though they're screaming over a concert that is not actually happening. She scrubs the counter fastidiously, speak-screaming into the oldish beige wall phone.)*

---

* A license to produce *Jennifer Who is Leaving* does not include a performance license for "Genie in a Bottle" by Christina Aguilera. The publisher and author suggest that the licensee contact ASCAP or BMI to ascertain the music publisher and contact such music publisher to license or acquire permission for performance of the song. If a license or permission is unattainable for "Genie in a Bottle," the licensee may not use the song in *Jennifer Who is Leaving* but should create an original composition in a similar style or use a similar song in the public domain. For further information, please see the Music and Third-Party Materials Use Note on page iii.

** A license to produce *Jennifer Who Is Leaving* does not include a license to publicly display any branded logos or trademarked images. Licensees must acquire rights for any logos and/or images or create their own

(Meanwhile, sitting in a wheelchair at a table in the corner eating a sugary powdered donut is **JOEY**, *eighties, wearing boring beige khakis and a thin sweater. He's making a giant mess, but* **NAN** *doesn't notice...yet. She will though.* **NAN** *never misses a goddamn trick, I tell you.)*

*(***JOEY** *keeps eating. He smears some sugar on his sweater. He still has more on his hands. He smears it on the table. He glances at* **NAN**. *She's occupied...)*

NAN. *(On the phone, not angry, just loud.)* NO, CHUCK, THE GLOVE COMPARTMENT OF THE SUBARU

THE SU. BAR. U.

THE SUBARU!

WELL I HAVE THE OLDSMOBILE SO, I MEAN

What OTHER glove compartment could there even BE?

Nothing has a GLOVE COMPARTMENT EXCEPT A CAR.

THEN PUT THE PHONE DOWN AND –

I AM NOT YELLING.

Just put the phone down and –

(She waits. She scrubs. A tough spot. She picks it with her nail. She scrubs more.)

WAS IT –

YOU'RE SURE IT'S NOT IN THE BASKET BY THE DOOR? BASKET. BY THE DOOR.

YES, THERE'S A BASKETBYTHE – YOU'RE POSITIVE?

Because last time we looked for three whole days – we had to GO TO MANNY for the special key and it cost fifty bucks to replace – NO IT *WAS* FIFTY!

IF YOU RECALL

And it was sitting in the basket by the door the entire time

EVEN THOUGH YOU CLAIMED YOU LOOKED

> (**JOEY** *starts to nibble off the edges of the donut. In a sort of weird OCD way.* **NAN** *perches on the counter.*)

Now don't get pissy with me, Mister. Because I'll tell you what!

I'll tell you a story about a woman. A woman who lay next to her husband LAST NIGHT seething as he slept because HE STEPPED OVER THE VACUUM

I vacuumed the whole house. Even the bath mat. I used the brush attachment on the baseboard! Then? I'm a scientist. I leave the vacuum out as an experiment. Would he put it away?! No! He stepped over the vacuum!

IT WAS SITTING RIGHT NEXT TO HIS SIDE OF THE BED

IT'S LIKE HE WANTS ME TO FALL ASLEEP HOMICIDAL –

NO CHUCK I DID NOT TAKE YOUR KEYS TO PUNISH YOU FOR THE VACUUM INCIDENT.

BECAUSE HONESTLY YOU LOSING YOUR KEYS IS A PUNISHMENT FOR ME MORE THAN ANYTHING AS WE CAN NOW SEE –

Did you see if it fell in the crack of the recliner?

THE RECLINER, I SAID.

NAN. *RECLINER.*

RE. CLINE. ER.

Tuesday night, nine p.m. –

You came in the door from the packie with a six-pack of Natty Ice, walked over my clean linoleum, took a tin of cashews, and you sat directly in that chair for the rest of the night, so I wouldn't be surprised –

Yes, I'll wait.

> (**JOEY** *is now carefully licking the entire donut. Almost dabbing his tongue on every part of the surface.* **NAN** *puts the phone down briefly, she rinses the rag she's been using to wipe the counter. She comes back to the phone.*)

Are you there?

Chuck?

> (*She scrubs/wipes with the phone resting in the crook of her neck. She waits. After a moment...*)

WELL WELL WELL

Uh huh

Yes.

I told you.

I can't believe you thought I TOOK YOUR KEYS.

I swear to god, Chuck.

Forty-two years of

"Where are my keys?"

"Where did you put the aspirin?"

"Where do we keep the peanut butter?"

"I can't find the nail clippers"

"Are my socks in the drawer?"

"Do you see the grill tongs?"

THE GRILL TONGS

THEY'RE RIGHT THERE THEY ARE RIGHT THERE

EVERYTHING IS ALWAYS RIGHT THERE

YOUR SOCKS ARE PROBABLY IN THE DRAWER THEY ARE RIGHT WHERE I PUT THEM AFTER I CLEANED THEM, WASHING THEM ONLY ON COLD AND THEN DRYING THEM SPECIFICALLY ON MEDIUM BECAUSE I DON'T WANT THEM TO STRETCH OUT

WHY DON'T YOU KNOW WHERE YOUR SOCKS ARE YOU ARE IN YOUR SIXTIES DO YOU HAVE SOME SORT OF COGNITIVE DELAY?

You are SO LUCKY you're cute.

> *(She grins. He's said something salacious. She's delighted...)*

Chuck! You're so! Chuck!

Chuck!

(Blushing.) Well, that sounds nice.

CHUCK I AM AT WORK.

That's not true I have a customer.

Yes, it's a man...

> *(She eyes **JOEY**, who is still dabbing his tongue on the donut. She makes a face.)*

...It's really not like that.

Uh huh

NAN. Uh huh

Well call them first to see if they're even open in this weather.

AND DON'T YOU DARE HANG OUT THERE AND TAKE A SINGLE SIP OF THAT SIX-PACK BEFORE YOU GET IN THE CAR

...We don't have an extra DIME if you bang it up again

I DON'T CARE WHOSE FAULT IT WAS, IT STILL COST US FOUR HUNDRED DOLLARS

I still owe Kim's daughter a wedding present, honestly.

She was very disappointed not to get anything.

Or maybe that was her face.

I can never tell, what with all the acne. Oof.

Or maybe it's psoriasis?

Chuck – was Kim's daughter the one with the skin thing, or –?

Well anyway, the groom seemed not to mind. Not like he's Tom Selleck, after all.

> (**NAN** *finishes the counter scrub, tossing the wipe into the sink. She glances over at* **JOEY**, *and then over at the bathroom.*)

Chuck, this is unprofessional, I have to go.

Yes.

Yes.

...Yes.

No.

YES, CHUCK. YES.

And there are some little Debbies in the cupboard. Twinkies too.

I said YES. No, you used the Swiss Cake Rolls last time you played because Gary's wife said, "No using quarters, the way you guys play."

Fine.

Alright.

I'll see you in a few hours, my-four-card trick. Four... five? Who cares?

NOT A SIP, REMEMBER.

Love you too.

> *(She giggles.)*

Alright, you.

> *(She hangs up.)*

(To herself.) Men!

> *(She looks over at **JOEY**, who is now carefully and completely licking his hands clean. He stuffs the rest of the donut he has also licked in his mouth.)*

JOEY. *(Defiantly, mouth full.)* This tastes like shit.

> *(**NAN** decides to ignore him. She rinses out the rag.)*

I said. THIS TASTES LIKE SHIT.

> *(**NAN** keeps ignoring him.)*

(Spewing donut a little.) SHIT SHIT SHIT SHIT

> *(This has **NAN**'s attention.)*

NAN. We don't need that kind of language, in here, Mister. This is a business.

JOEY. Starbucks is a business. This is a DUMP –

*(**NAN** marches over and cleans up the errant pieces of donut. She also removes another one that was sitting there as well.)*

JOEY. GIMME MY DONUT

NAN. You said it tastes like / shit!

JOEY. / That is a DIFFERENT DONUT Jesus H Christ

NAN. You really are *a piece of work*, I tell ya.

(She hands him back the donut. He takes a bite pointedly.)

JOEY. *(Dramatically.)* MMMMMMMMM

(Then…referring the pop song playing:)

I hate this song.

NAN. Oh? It's just the mix that plays.

JOEY. I hate it.

NAN. Well, I'm not supposed to turn it off.

JOEY. I HATE IT.

NAN. It's almost over.

*(**NAN** sighs. **NAN** goes back to the sink, starts filling up a giant industrial coffee carafe to brew a new pot.)*

JOEY. I HATE IT. IT SOUNDS LIKE SH–

*(**NAN** turns and glares at him. He better not say "shit." He doesn't. She turns back to scrubbing.)*

(Whispering.) Shit.

*(**JOEY** smiles to himself. **NAN** pauses scrubbing and gets a stack of foldable donut containers.)*

What are those?

NAN. These are how you're gonna earn your keep.

JOEY. My keep?

NAN. Yeah, you know, 'keep' – like / you're gonna earn your way –

JOEY. / I KNOW WHAT KEEP MEANS I'M OLD I KNOW MORE THAN YOU, JESUS H CHRIST

NAN. Alright, alright. But. You're gonna be here awhile waiting for that truck, so you're gonna keep busy so you don't drive me up the goddamn wall.

(She plops the unfolded boxes in front of him.)

Here. Like this.

(She shows him. It's easy. He picks one up. He does it wrong.)

(Leaning over to correct.) No...like this.

(He does it wrong again.)

Almost, not quite –

(She corrects, again.)

(He aggressively folds it wrong.)

(She realizes.)

(Oh.)

(This is on purpose.)

(A little impressed.) You little pissah. Alright, then. You're lucky I respect my elders or I'd throw you out in the storm.

JOEY. *(Bored.)* You would not.

NAN. I would!

JOEY. Nuh uh.

NAN. Don't test me, pal.

> (**JOEY** *throws the box in his hands on the ground. Just as* **JENNIFER**, *mid-forties, enters from the bathroom. She's wearing scrubs with a fun ZANY pattern.*)

JENNIFER. JOE! Do NOT throw things!

> (**JOEY** *starts to cry. Crocodile tears.*)

Sorry, he knows better.

JOEY. *(Still fake crying.)* No I don't! I dooooon't!

NAN. He always like this?

JENNIFER. Well –

JOEY. *(Still tears.)* YEAH I AM

> (**JENNIFER** *rolls her eyes. Picks up the box. She glances at the door.*)

JENNIFER. *(To* **NAN**.*)* I can fold them while we wait. I'm so sorry to squat here. I promise, we're leaving.

NAN. It's fine. Place'll be dead tonight. Deliveries are all halted because'a the storm, and that's who mostly comes in here at night.

> (**JENNIFER** *goes and looks out the window, a little anxiously.*)

JENNIFER. Is this the last stop before the bridge?

NAN. Yep. In the summer all the, you know, *city men* – on the way to P-Town...they come in here with their mesh shirts and crazy earrings. I love it. They're a hoot. It's kinda the Key West of the Northeast.

JOEY. I WANNA GO HOME

JENNIFER. *(Shielding her eyes to peer through.)* I know, Joe.

JOEY. YOU SAID THERE WAS A MOVIE

  I WANNA GO BACK TO THE CENTER

JENNIFER. I hear you.

JOEY. FUCK YOU.

> **(JENNIFER** *sighs.* **NAN** *looks slightly scandalized.)*

JENNIFER. I'm so sorry / again

NAN. / He's really got a potty mouth, huh?

JENNIFER. You should see what he says to the aides he DOESN'T like.

NAN. I can't even imagine!

JOEY. *(Proudly.)* I'm incorrigible.

JENNIFER. *(Fishing out a pen and a piece of crumpled paper from her purse.)* Here, draw a picture, Joey.

JOEY. A PICTURE??!?!?

JENNIFER. Yes, maybe a self-portrait / or something

JOEY. / I HAVE CATARACTS YOU ARE SO INSENSITIVE

JENNIFER. Okay, fine! Suit yourself!

JOEY. Draw a g-damn PICTURE – I'm a g-damn ADULT. Jesus H Christ. I used to have a JOB. I contributed to SOCIETY. No one has a JOB these days.

JENNIFER. We both have jobs, Joey. She works here and you're my / job –

JOEY. / NOT BY THE LOOKS OF IT. You're sitting eating donuts and she's making the customers do all the work!

> *(He throws another box.)*

JENNIFER. *(To* **NAN,** *as she picks up the box.)* I'm so sorry, he gets especially anxious when he's outside of his comfort zone –

JOEY. I CAN HEAR YOU, DUMMY.

> *(***JOEY*** stops. He stares at her. He is kind of into it.)*

NAN. *(Raising her voice.)* Now listen, you old goat. Knock it off or I'll lock you in the bathroom for the rest of the time you're here. You get me?

> *(It's important to note she would never do this. And he knows that. But she has laid down the law and he respects a bitch who yells.* **NAN** *turns away.)*

(Calmly to **JENNIFER.***)* Would you like a coffee or a choc-accino?

JENNIFER. Do they still make those?

NAN. Discontinued in 2009. But if you know the right people...

JENNIFER. *(A little stunned.)* A choc-accino sounds nice.

NAN. You want whipped cream?

It's been a tough night, you deserve a little treat. We all deserve a little treat now and then.

> *(***NAN** *starts to make the coffee.* **JOEY** *makes his presence known.)*

JOEY. *(Singing.)*
JENNY JENNY
LOOKS LIKE A PENNY
JENNY JENNY
LOOKS LIKE A PENNY

JENNIFER. *(Weary.)* Joey. Please. Take it down a notch, okay?

JOEY. *(Singing.)*
JENNY HENNY
SHE LIKES LENNY
JENNY KENNY
SHE LIKES LENNY

NAN. *(From behind the counter.)* Lenny?

JENNIFER. He likes to rhyme.

NAN. *(From behind the counter.)* ...Okay.

JOEY. *(Chanting.)* FRITZ

TITS

FRITZ

TITS

FRITZ

TITS!

> **(JENNIFER** *gives* **JOEY** *a "knock it off" look.*
> *He grins. Satan. Truly.* **NAN** *comes around*
> *the counter with a coffee for* **JENNIFER.)**

Where's mine?

NAN. You haven't earned it.

> **(JOEY** *sticks his tongue out and* **NAN** *bites at*
> *him. He recoils in fear.* **JENNIFER** *smiles.)*

My mom had Alzheimer's.

JOEY. I DON'T HAVE / THAT

NAN. *(Raising her voice above* **JOEY***'s.)* / So I get that
they're difficult sometimes.

JENNIFER. *(Smiling weakly.)* It's the job.

And.

Some of them are sweet.

JOEY. *(Proudly.)* Not me! HAHAHAHAH

> (**NAN** *glares at him. He stops. He's now a touch afraid of her. Good.*)

NAN. *(To* **JENNIFER**.*)* You shouldn't let him talk to you like that.

(To **JOEY**.*)* Don't talk back to this nice lady who takes care of you.

JOEY. That ugly witch?

WITCH

BITCH

WITCH

BITCH

JENNIFER. I'm so sorry we're bothering you. This is…

I just needed to pull over right away.

NAN. It's not a problem, honey. Keeps it a little more exciting. I like when there's action. Makes the shift go by faster. The night shift is very quiet.

JENNIFER. Tell me about it.

> (**JOEY** *screams like "I'm not quiet."*)

JOEY. AHHHHHHHHHHHHHHH

(Then he gets bored and stops.)

NAN. *(Scrubbing the counters.)* So. What are you two doing out in this crazy weather? All the way from Lynn?

JENNIFER. *(Distracted.)* Oh…what?

NAN. The logo on the side of the van says Lynn –

JENNIFER. Oh, just, on our way back from his doctor in Boston.

I went the wrong way.

NAN. I'll say! About an hour and a half the wrong way...

JENNIFER. ...I wasn't using the GPS. I thought I knew where I was going.

NAN. Oh I been there! And my husband, Chuck – he never uses it. He's SUCH a man. Can NEVER ask for directions.

JENNIFER. Ugh, yeah, Bill's the same way.

NAN. That's your husband?

JENNIFER. *(Holding up her ring hand.)* Twenty years. Well, it's more like twenty-one now –

NAN. *(Re: the ring.)* Wow! What a rock! Fancy!

JENNIFER. Yeah, well, his mother bought it for him from a pawn shop. She wanted grandkids before she died.

NAN. Oh, I'm sorry.

JENNIFER. Don't worry, she's still alive.

JOEY. *SAME*

NAN. Chuck's mother died in 2009 and –

JOEY. *(Interrupting.)* I'M BORED

NAN. Who cares?

JOEY. *(To* **JENNIFER.***)* You gonna let her speak to me like that?

JENNIFER. *(A small smile.)* Yes.

NAN. I'll speak to you however I like and so will she!

JOEY. No because I'll tell on her. I saw her smoking a cigarette in her car last week DURING BUSINESS HOURS –

JENNIFER. *(To* **NAN.***)* It was my lunch break –

JOEY. PROVE IT

JENNIFER. *(Eye roll.)* Joey –

JOEY. She steals, too, I've seen it. I'm gonna file a REPORT

NAN. Oh yeah?

JOEY. YEAH

I KNOW MY RIGHTS

JENNIFER. Okay, Joe, fine, file a report, then.

JOEY. I WILL AND YOU'LL BE SORRY

HAHAHAHAHAHHAHAHAHAHA

HAHAHA

> (**NAN** *watches him evil laugh for a minute. Then he gets bored. Plays dead. The* **WOMEN** *look at him deadpan with essentially no reaction. He peeks at them.* **NAN** *shrugs, moves on casually.*)

NAN. So you have kids?

JENNIFER. Two.

NAN. Boys? Girls?

JENNIFER. Girls. Both of 'em.

NAN. Girls! You're so lucky. Three boys.

Boys are the WORST.

JOEY. Fuck you.

JENNIFER. *(Warning.)* Joey...

> (**JOEY** *sulks.*)

I always wanted boys.

> (*Throughout the next section, it is helpful if* **NAN** *is doing tasks around the shop. She is not confessing, or trying to get pity. Because, frankly, it should be noted, probably even earlier than this, that* **NAN** *chats. It's not*

heavy conversation, please. She's just an oversharer. She's the woman in line who comments on your groceries even if you have headphones in.)

NAN. They leave their sports gear everywhere! It was always baseball gloves and hockey sticks and lacrosse helmets and mouth guards and, geez, by the time they were through I felt like I lived in a Sports Authority, honestly.

JENNIFER. *(Trying to be polite.)* Ah, well, girls leave their things around too. If I had a nickel for every time the vacuum got jammed on a hair elastic.

NAN. Oh! Wanna see a picture of 'em?

> (**NAN** *pulls out a sort of gaudy locket from around her neck.)*

JENNIFER. Of...?

NAN. My boys!

JENNIFER. Oh...um / I –

NAN. *(Running over and opening the locket.)* / C.J. – that's Charles Jr. – looks JUST like Chuck, Timothy – looks like my brother, and Sean – he looks like no one, so go figure! All grown now. Every time they call I keep beggin' for grandkids, but it's not looking good. / It's really NOT looking good.

JENNIFER. ...I'm sorry?

> (**NAN** *puts her locket away, continues her deep counter clean.)*

NAN. I'm not. It is what it is. The only time I hate it is when Chuck and I go to bowling league on Tuesdays and this woman – Grace Van der Bil is her name, though who cares – she brings her little Grandson Ethan and he is just...oh he's an ANGEL. And she's IN LOVE with him. So that seems nice. But otherwise, I'm fine.

NAN. It's their life, and I get it. Kids are hard.

JENNIFER. They sure / are.

JOEY. / I'M BORED

AHHHHHHHHHHHHHHHHHHH

JENNIFER. Joey, take a nap!

JOEY. Nap?

I don't need a nap!

I'M A G-DAMN ADULT –

(**NAN** *goes over and shoves another donut in his mouth. He chews.*)

JENNIFER. Thanks.

NAN. No prob, Bob.

(*There's a pause.* **JOEY** *chews.* **JENNIFER** *glances out the window then looks back at* **NAN**. *She doesn't know what to say. After a moment, she ventures…*)

JENNIFER. I didn't used to think I wanted kids. But you know, here we are. So maybe the boys'll change their minds.

NAN. Oh ho ho ho! Oh no. I don't think so.

C.J. is very career-focused. No serious relationships.

JENNIFER. Career?

NAN. Barback. Demanding hours.

JENNIFER. I'll bet.

(**NAN** *crosses back behind the counter and finishes filling the first coffee pot. She starts to fill the other.*)

NAN. Timmy is a little bit of a ladies' man, so we'll see. He's thirty-three, so I betcha he'll settle down soon. And well, Sean is…well, he's a work in progress, but we're very proud. He doesn't live in the basement anymore so, thank god Chuck's got his man cave back!

JENNIFER. Hmph. I'd love a man cave.

NAN. *(Laughing.)* Oh god, you and me both! You and me both, sister. You know, C.J. and Timmy – I never REALLY worry about them. Sean was always different, though. More fragile.

JENNIFER. My youngest is too.

NAN. *(A light sigh.)* Sean always hung out with the wrong people, too. I never liked his friends. But you know, the last year or two has been nice to see. He's been totally clean. He even got me a birthday present. 'Course I hated the color – it was one of them infinity scarves.

JENNIFER. Well, it's the thought that counts, I guess.

NAN. Absolutely. Absolutely. Also, I could return it, so there's that.

JENNIFER. Oh…good.

NAN. *(Just sharing, not looking for sympathy.)* Yup. We had some dark times. OF COURSE Chuck wanted to give up, but you know – a mother never does. I never did. Even when, oh wow, it was awful. I cried myself to sleep for YEARS. We'd spent our life savings on the third rehab. We didn't have anything else. But then Chuck's uncle passed – Thank God – and we used that money to give it another shot – Chuck didn't want to, but I begged and pleaded. I told him we had to save my baby. And this time – so far – it's taken.

JENNIFER. That's great.

NAN. *(A laugh.)* Sean says one day at a time. He gets so mad when I ask how it's going. Says I'm henpecking or nagging or whatever – but I say, when I give up my whole life for you, I get to ASK HOW IT'S GOING.

*(She laughs, genuinely for a bit. **JENNIFER** smiles or maybe even laughs a little too, to be polite.)*

JOEY. *(Interrupting loudly, mouth full.)* What, was he a drunk?

JENNIFER. Joey!

NAN. *(Laughing.)* Oh god, I wish. I WISH. Heroin. Real common these days. In my day we smoked pot and ate an Italian sub, but I mean, I guess the world is more complicated now.

JENNIFER. Ha.

*(A tiny pause. **NAN** looks over at **JENNIFER**, a slight break in her task but then –)*

JOEY. Oh please, don't tell me about how complicated it is now. I was here when they invented cars.

JENNIFER. No, you weren't.

JOEY. Prove it.

NAN. Speaking of cars! Jennifer, want to call the towing company again? Heckle them a little. Those boys over there are slow. If you caught 'em in the middle of their card game –

JOEY. I wanna play a game. Give me your phone, I wanna play Words with Friends.

NAN. *(Snidely, a little joke.)* You have friends?

JOEY. IT'S THE NAME OF THE GAME

JENNIFER. Joey, my phone died, I told you that –

JOEY. NO YOU DIDN'T

JENNIFER. I did you just don't remember.

JOEY. WELL WHOSE FAULT IS THAT?

JENNIFER. *(To* **NAN.***)* Yeah. I should. I should try the truck again. See if they can come faster.

NAN. Knock yourself out –

> *(The jingle of the shop door. In comes* **LILI**, *seventeen, bundled up to the max. She's in a huff. She whips around the counter.)*

Lili –

LILI. God, it's horrible out there!

NAN. Didn't you get my message not to come in? I didn't want you driving in these conditions!

LILI. My stupid Dad drove me –

JOEY. RUDE RUDE RUDE

LILI. Who are you?

JOEY. I don't know.

NAN. They're stuck – but I called twice! I even had Nadine show me how to text you!

LILI. Well, serves my Dad right because he confiscated my phone.

NAN. Why? What did you do?

LILI. Back talk. APPARENTLY.

NAN. Well, you know, you have to understand, your mom and dad, they've worked so hard to make sure you –

LILI. OH MY GOD I KNOW.

> *(***LILI*** storms off into the back [presumably to the break room].)*

NAN. Lili. Her mother Maria is the daytime Shift Manager. She's worked here, god, I don't know. I mean she hired ME, haha! So sweet. She's VERY little. Extremely petite. Honestly, it's a little shocking. She comes up behind me sometimes and –

(**NAN** *makes a face like "it's scary!" Just as* **LILI** *storms back in, fastening on her nametag, sighing.* **NAN** *quickly stops gossiping.*)

NAN. Lili, meet Jennifer and Joey –

JENNIFER. Hi.

LILI. *(Begrudgingly.)* Hi.

JOEY. Hi blah blah hi blah

JENNIFER. Sorry about him, he's ornery at nighttime.

NAN. Just nighttime?

JOEY. *(Proudly.)* Yeah

NAN. *(To* **LILI**.*)* Their van broke down. They're waiting for a tow truck.

LILI. Well good luck getting one in this shithole town.

> (**JOEY** *claps.*)

JOEY. SHIT SHIT SHIT

NAN. *(To* **JOEY**.*)* HUSHUP YOU.

> (**JOEY** *mutes himself, but still claps and mouths "Shit shit shit."*)

(To **LILI**.*)* Now, why are you being fresh with your parents?

LILI. I told them I didn't have time for this *stupid* job, but they made me anyway and now I'm wicked STRESSED OUT.

NAN. Welcome to adulthood.

LILI. I'm not an adult.

NAN. Geez, when I was your age, I couldn't WAIT for people to mistake me as an adult. I wore eyeliner and everything.

JOEY. Disgusting.

NAN. Now THAT I agree with ya on, Joe. Gave me so many eye goobers. It was a SIGHT.

(*To* **LILI**.) Why are you stressed?

LILI. The SATs are tomorrow and I didn't take enough practice tests and my practice scores weren't good enough to get me into Oberlin.

NAN. Oberlin?! You wanna go all the way to California?

LILI. Oberlin is in Ohio, Nan.

NAN. You wanna go all the way to Ohio?! What's wrong with UMass?

LILI. *Everyone* goes to UMass.

NAN. And everyone is doing just fine.

LILI. ...

JOEY. I went to G.W.

JENNIFER. No you didn't.

JOEY. Prove it.

NAN. Oh honey, are they even gonna HAVE the test tomorrow? This weather. I bet it'll get postponed.

LILI. (*She had never thought of that.*) What?! REALLY?! You think???

NAN. Probably.

> (**LILI** *looks at* **JENNIFER**. *She wants another adult to weigh in.*)

JENNIFER. Oh. Yeah, maybe?

LILI. Oh my god!

Oh my god –

How will I know?

NAN. There must be some hotline or something, don't you think?

LILI. Probably, but I can't check my confirmation without my PHONE ARGGGGGHHHHH MY STUPID DADDDDDDDD AH / HHHH

JOEY. / AHHHHHHHHHHHHHH

JENNIFER. Joe. Knock it off.

LILI. Nan, can I go and check in the back on the gateway?

NAN. If you can get it to work, sure.

LILI. YESSSS!!!

(**LILI** *runs off to the break room.*)

NAN. *(Shouting after her.)* Don't you dare punch / in!

JOEY. / I have to pee.

JENNIFER. *(Getting up.)* Alright, let's get you in there.

JOEY. NOW.

JENNIFER. I'm going!

JOEY. NOW NOW

JENNIFER. I hear you –

JOEY. *(Singing.)*
MILK MILK LEMONADE
ROUND THE CORNER FUDGE IS MADE

NAN. Joe! That's nasty!

JOEY. *(Spurred on.)*
MILK MILK LEMONADE
ROUND THE CORNER FUDGE IS MADE

JENNIFER. *(Wheeling him into the bathroom.)* ENOUGH.

(*She wheels him into the bathroom. He continues singing from behind the door.*)

JOEY. *(Loudly from behind the door.)*
MILK MILK LEMONADE
ROUND THE CORNER FUDGE IS MADE

AND YER GONNA CLEAN IT

HAHAHAHAHAHAHA

> *(Outside the bathroom, **NAN** sighs. She disappears for a moment. The stage is empty. The pop mix still plays. The following happens behind the bathroom door, but we hear it all.)*

(Shouting.) OW.

JENNIFER. You're fine. Stop wiggling.

JOEY. OW!

ABUSE

OW

JENNIFER. JOEY. Stop it. I'm trying to –

JOEY. *(Fake crying.)* OWWWWWWWW

JENNIFER. Shhh shhhh you're okay, please. Enough with the crocodile tears.

PLEASE. Just PLEASE.

PLEASE

PLEASE

> *(**JOEY** cries. **JENNIFER** begs.)*

Please, Joey. Please. Not today. I just. I can't. I can't.

> *(She's losing her grip. **JOEY** cries louder.)*

JOEY. LET ME HELP YOU.

JOEY. NO!

JENNIFER. Joey, come on – I'm tired, please.

JOEY. I'M TIRED

ME! I AM

I AM THE TIRED ONE

JENNIFER. Okay, fine. FINE.

> (**JENNIFER** *comes out, slamming the door behind her. She sits down at the table closest to the bathroom. She puts her head down. She takes a breath. Another. Another. It's okay. She's okay. Pull it together, Jennifer.*)

> (*When she looks up:*)

> (*Suddenly and without warning, she quickly puts on her jacket and zips up. She runs to the bathroom door and listens. Quiet. She grabs her purse and runs to the outside door. She stops. Places her head on the glass. Breathes. She's about to push open the door when...*)

JOEY. (*From inside.*) Help

Help help

Help help

Jenny help

Milk Milk

Lemonade

> (**JENNIFER** *bites her lip. She rocks herself back and forth a tiny bit. After an agonizing moment, she realizes herself. She quickly exhales, leaving the door, taking her jacket off and throwing it on the chair.*)

JENNIFER. (*Calling to* **JOEY.**) Coming.

(She goes back in the bathroom.)

(Behind the door.) You done messin' around?

JOEY. No.

JENNIFER. Come on, then.

> *(She clearly resumes helping him. We hear a flush.* **NAN** *returns from the back room with a full bucket of water and a mop.)*

NAN. *(To herself.)* Darn salt everywhere.

> *(She goes to each table [except the one* **JOEY** *and* **JENNIFER** *have been using] and flips up the chairs to prep for mopping. Her keys jangle.)*

> *(She starts to mop. She gets in a rhythm. She mops a section and then slides the bucket. Mop, slide. Mop, slide. It's not totally unenjoyable. A song like "Dancing Queen" or something immediately recognizable and fun for multiple generations comes on in the mix.* Something that could have been Jennifer's favorite song in high school. She might whistle with it. Mop, slide. Mop, slide.)*

> *(She does a little dance move, which she quickly masks as the bathroom door opens.* **JENNIFER** *wheels* **JOEY** *out. She runs his chair into the mop bucket accidentally. The mop water goes everywhere.)*

---

* A license to produce *Jennifer Who is Leaving* does not include a performance license for "Dancing Queen" by ABBA. The publisher and author suggest that the licensee contact ASCAP or BMI to ascertain the music publisher and contact such music publisher to license or acquire permission for performance of the song. If a license or permission is unattainable for "Dancing Queen," the licensee may not use the song in *Jennifer Who is Leaving* but should create an original composition in a similar style or use a similar song in the public domain. For further information, please see the Music and Third-Party Materials Use Note on page iii.

JOEY. HAHAHAHAHAHAHAHAHA / HAHAHAHAHA

(He meanly laughs throughout the following:)

JENNIFER. Oh shoot! Shoot! Nan!

*(**NAN** is already on the scene with the brown rolls of paper towel. She's in action. She's like a cat. She's like a fat stage manager who suddenly looks like a ninja when something spills. **JENNIFER** grabs some. They make a barrier to contain the water.)*

NAN. Now we dab.

*(At one point, **LILI** comes out, sees they're doing that, and quietly disappears into the break room to avoid helping. **JOEY** sees.)*

JOEY. HEY HEY HEY

*(He points frantically at **LILI**.)*

JENNIFER. Joe, calm down!

*(**JENNIFER** falls to her bottom. **JOEY** laughs more.)*

*(**NAN** stands and grabs the mop. She pauses for a second, commands him, like a dog – a finger in his face.)*

NAN. NO.

*(He sulks. **NAN** and **JENNIFER** are seeing the light at the end of the tunnel. The phone rings. The landline.)*

(Holding a pile of dripping towels.) Shoot!

I'm coming!

JOEY. You missed a spot.

NAN. Coming!

JOEY. They can't hear you dummy.

> (**NAN** *sort of frantically dashes around with the towels,* **JENNIFER** *intercepts and takes them the rest of the way to the trash. She goes back to mop some more as* **NAN** *answers the phone.* **JOEY** *starts to sing loudly to himself over the call.*)

NAN. *(On the phone.)* Hello! You've reached your home for donuts on Cranberry Highway –

Chuck!

Jesus Chuck, I was in the middle of –

JENNIFER. I'm so sorry! I didn't see it over his chair!

NAN. Shortest game in –

Put it at four hundred.

Yep.

Thirty minutes.

No.

No.

> *(Pause.)*

No.

I told you it would be that long.

Yes.

Yes.

> *(Pause.)*

---

* A license to produce *Jennifer Who is Leaving* does not include a performance license for any third-party or copyrighted music. Licensees should create an original composition or use music in the public domain. For further information, please see the Music and Third-Party Materials Use Note on page iii.

NAN. Yes I did.

First drawer on the right.

...no the RIGHT. RIGHT.

No, that's the left.

BECAUSE I KNOW WHAT'S IN THE DRAWERS, THAT'S THE LEFT ONE SANDWICH BAGS ARE IN THE LEFT ONE AND THE RIGHT HAS –

Yes.

Mmmm hmmm.

(She rolls her eyes at **JENNIFER** *like "Can you believe men?"* **JENNIFER** *mops, she smiles weakly.* **JOEY** *is no longer singing. He's shredding a napkin.)*

I left you an index card with it all on –

Okay, the onions are already chopped in the produce drawer.

Add 'em on at the end.

I DON'T KNOW, IT'S TO TASTE, CHUCK TO YOUR OWN TASTE

Now don't leave it in there after you take what you want.

It's supposed to be TWO dinners.

So cover it with Saran wrap –

FINE ALUMINUM FOIL, though honestly, I do not understand why you hate Saran wrap so –

It does TOO stick. It sticks to the sides –

Well, you have to be careful, Chuck, of course. You have to be CAREFUL.

But either way, make sure you don't just leave it in the oven to dry out til I'm home at four.

Chuck, it's always four.

Always.

(*Suddenly.*) HI BRANDON HI SWEETIE PIE

HI BRANDON

GOOD BOY

SWEET BOY

WHO'S A GOOD BOY

WHO IS

YOU ARE

(*To Chuck.*) Is he wagging his tail?

Can he hear me?

Should you put me on speaker –?

THEN LIGHT THE PILOT LIGHT

Did he eat dinner?

BRANDON.

THE DOG.

DID YOU FEED HIM?

Did you give him the pill?

FOR THE VIRAL WARTS ON HIS PAW, CHUCK

The lazy Susan by the door –

Because you're supposed to give it to him after his after dinner walk –

You did WALK HIM, didn't you –

WELL I DON'T KNOW ANYMORE, I WOULD HAVE THOUGHT THAT ABOUT THE PILL TOO

Okay.

OKAY.

NAN. Okay.

No, put it way in the back of his throat and then rub his nose.

No, his NOSE.

Hahahaha – well that would be quite something.

Just his nose, though.

Then check around the floor to make sure he swallowed –

Yes.

Yes.

I know.

Yes.

Yes…

Four hundred! Jesus, Chuck. FOUR HUNDRED DEGREES.

No, that will just burn it.

Thirty minutes.

Okay, sure, check it at twenty-five

> *(She rolls her eyes at **JENNIFER**, who smiles a little.)*

Okay, sweetie.

Uh huh.

Okay.

Okay.

I love you, too.

(Flirtatious.) Stop, I have customers.

FOUR, CHUCK. IT'S ALWAYS FOUR.

I know, I know

Okay.

Love you, too.

Buh bye.

> (**JOEY** *is now shredding a napkin and eating the paper.*)

(Conspiratorially as she takes over the mop.) So I'm doing this little experiment with Chuck. Where I make him make his own dinner on the nights I work. Because it's ridiculous, I work seven p.m. to four a.m. So I go home, and I'm amped up and so I don't go to bed til six or seven, then honestly, I'm a slug, so I sleep til one or two, and then I only have four hours to clean the house, grocery shop, you know, and now he's retired. So I thought he could pitch in!

> (**JOEY** *starts throwing the tiny pieces of napkin on the ground.* **JENNIFER** *wordlessly goes over and picks them up. He casually keeps adding to it.*)

So I made a deal with myself, I said, NAN! You gotta stop chewing his meat for him.

JOEY. EW

NAN. I gotta stop acting like he can't do anything himself. So I make these casseroles and fajitas – well, like enchiladas – who cares – and things, and I put these index cards taped on top of them in the freezer or fridge and he has to follow the instructions and make them HIMSELF.

JENNIFER. Smart.

NAN. RIGHT!? It's wicked easy, so he has no excuses, pop 'em right in the oven, you know. So now I'm totally hands off, he's all on his own. AND! I get to eat the dinner HE makes when I get home. I HAVE GAMED THE SYSTEM!

JENNIFER. Sounds perfect.

JOEY. I'm bored

JENNIFER. I can get your bird book from the car

JOEY. DO YOU SEE ANY BIRDS IT'S THE DEAD OF WINTER

JENNIFER. Fine! Jeez, it's your book.

JOEY. Some sick g-damn idea of a YANKEE SWAP present

I never even WANTED it.

JENNIFER. Okay, fine, do nothing then. See if I care.

> (**JOEY** *sulks.* **LILI** *peeks back out. The mop is gone. Coast is clear.*)

NAN. Did you find the number?

LILI. Yeah. Can I call?

NAN. Did you punch in?

LILI. You told me not to.

NAN. Then fine. Use that one.

> (**LILI** *crosses to the beige landline.*)

If you hear a beep, take it, it might be Manny at the towing company.

> (**LILI** *rolls her eyes. She picks up the phone and dials.*)

> (*She speaks loudly into the phone.*)

LILI. SPEAK TO A REPRESENTATIVE

NAN. *(To herself.)* I'll KILL her if she doesn't answer the beep.

> (**NAN** *mouths "answer the beep" and* **LILI** *mouths back "I will!"* **NAN** *is satisfied. She looks over at* **JENNIFER,** *who is sipping her coffee, maybe staring into space.*)

JOEY. I'M BORED

NAN. Only boring people are bored.

JOEY. Ah, fuck you.

NAN. F yourself, Mister.

JOEY. "F yourself, Mister." Good one blah blah blah

> (**NAN** *shrugs him off.*)

NAN. Jennifer, I'm SO RUDE.

JENNIFER. *(Snapping back into it.)* Oh, what?

NAN. I went on and on about the boys!

JENNIFER. Oh, that's / fine –

NAN. / Tell me about your girls.

JENNIFER. Oh. Well. They're all grown up now.

NAN. Names! Ages!

JOEY. "Names. Ages." BLAH BLAH BLAH

JENNIFER. *(Too tired to argue with him.)* Jessica is twenty-one and Emmy is nineteen.

LILI. Ugh this hold music is burning my ears.

NAN. It must be nice having girls.

JOEY. YOU ALREADY SAID THAT

NAN. What's your husband do?

JENNIFER. He's in construction.

NAN. Oooo! A craftsman!

JENNIFER. I mean...

He works hard, I guess.

NAN. Ha! Isn't it funny? We always say "he works hard" – everyone says that about Chuck, too. But you never hear anyone say that about us!

JENNIFER. True.

NAN. YA NEVER HEAR ANYONE SAY "She mothers hard" or "She cleans hard."

JOEY. TO BE A DEVIL'S ADVOCATE

THAT SOUNDS RIDICULOUS

>*(He grabs Jennifer's coffee and dumps it on the ground. **JENNIFER** mindlessly kneels down and cleans it up.)*

NAN. You know what else sounds ridiculous? When you men say you're playing DEVIL'S ADVOCATE. What a gift to argue for the *fun* of it! What a gift! I don't have that kind of time!

JOEY. *(Genuinely confused.)* HUH

JENNIFER. *(Tired.)* Joey, hush.

LILI. *(On the phone, someone has picked up!)* HI HI Hello – um I'm taking the test at center 00356 and...

NAN. Tell her the weather is awful!

>*(**LILI** motions to **NAN** to be quiet. **NAN** waits. **LILI** listens.)*

LILI. *(On the phone.)* The weather is...inclement. So I was wondering if that means they'll cancel the test.

>*(**LILI** listens. It doesn't look good.)*

NAN. I mean they MUST, it's absolutely HAZARDOUS out there –

>*(**LILI** motions to **NAN** to shut up again.)*

JOEY. I'M BORED

NAN. Zip it.

>*(**NAN** motions to **JOEY** to shut up. **JENNIFER** gives him a warning look. He sulks.)*

JOEY. *(Whining.)* I wanted to watch the movie.

LILI. 02576

JENNIFER. *(Eyeing* **NAN**.*)* We have to

Wait for the tow truck.

> (**LILI** *writes a number on a napkin.* **NAN**
> *leans over to see.)*

JOEY. WHAT TRUCK

JENNIFER. The tow truck –

JOEY. SOMETHING IS WRONG WITH THE VAN???

NAN. Joey! Shhhh!

LILI. *(On the phone, repeating back.)* 800-918-0865?

JENNIFER. *(Rubbing her head, is a migraine coming on?)* Yes Joey... Remember?

JOEY. NO I DON'T REMEMBER! I HAVE DEMENTIA

JENNIFER. *(To* **NAN**.*)* Well as soon as it's fixed, we're leaving.

JOEY. Well hurry up!

JENNIFER. Shhh, Joe.

LILI. Thank you. Okay. Thanks.

Yes.

Okay.

Thanks.

Goodbye.

> (She hangs up the phone and slams her head
> down on the counter.)

NAN. Not good?

LILI. I have to call this stupid number in the morning and they won't call it 'til then, but it's unlikely she said they rarely cancel, but I'm welcomed to reschedule for a FEE.

NAN. I'm SURE your parents would pay to reschedule –

LILI. NO MY FATHER IS TRYING TO TEACH ME RESPONSIBILITY SO HE'S MAKING ME PAY FOR ALL COLLEGE RELATED EXPENSES IT IS WHY I HAVE THIS INANE JOB

NAN. Hey now! It's not all bad. You get unlimited donuts –

JOEY. They taste like shit.

> (**NAN** *shoots him a glare.*)

LILI. They really do.

NAN. Come on, now, Lili. You'll be great on the test, you're a great student.

LILI. Nan, I know that, but the test it's like...you have to know certain *strategies*. It's like a game. And I didn't prepare –

NAN. Oh come on. I don't even remember if I ever TOOK the SATs and I'm fine!

> (**LILI** *doesn't say anything.* **JENNIFER** *clocks it.*)

Isn't it true if you just answer C, you pass?

LILI. (*A little rude, maybe.*) The test isn't pass-fail, Nan.

NAN. Well, excuse me for living. Jennifer, did you take the SATs?

JENNIFER. Yup.

JOEY. AND LOOK WHERE THAT GOT YA

NAN. Well, that's rude, Joey.

JOEY. Prove it.

JENNIFER. I wasn't much of a student, honestly. But I remember them telling us the biggest tip was to take our time and *relax*.

(She looks pointedly at **LILI**. **LILI** *doesn't roll her eyes, but she wants to.)*

My girls just took them – only a few years ago. Emmy especially did really well.

LILI. How many prep classes did they take?

JENNIFER. None.

LILI. *(Knowing.)* Ohhh, a tutor.

JENNIFER. Nope. Well, I think Emmy did a couple sessions at her school in the guidance office? Maybe?

LILI. *(A touch withering/snide…just a touch.)* Well, I need to break 1400.

> *(There's a silence for a second.* **LILI** *falls into a sulk and* **JENNIFER** *goes quiet. A song like Whitney Houston's "I Wanna Dance With Somebody" comes on the mix.* **NAN**, *trying to lighten the mood, sways a little. Mouths the lyrics…just a little, to herself. She eyes* **LILI**. *She dances a little over to her, super dorky.* **JENNIFER** *smiles a touch.* **NAN** *starts to really sing a bit, trying to make* **LILI** *laugh.* **LILI** *covers her ears. No way.* **NAN** *gives up on her and solos a little, grabbing a mop or duster or something to use as a mic. She sings herself over to* **JENNIFER**, *who laughs, a little embarrassed.* **NAN** *is having a fun time,*

---

* A license to produce *Jennifer Who is Leaving* does not include a performance license for "I Wanna Dance With Somebody" by Whitney Houston. The publisher and author suggest that the licensee contact ASCAP or BMI to ascertain the music publisher and contact such music publisher to license or acquire permission for performance of the song. If a license or permission is unattainable for "I Wanna Dance With Somebody," the licensee may not use the song in *Jennifer Who is Leaving* but should create an original composition in a similar style or use a similar song in the public domain. For further information, please see the Music and Third-Party Materials Use Note on page iii.

singing to herself and **JENNIFER** *suddenly sees* **NAN**...*she's a little inspired. She joins in too. As the chorus hits,* **JENNIFER** *and* **NAN** *team up to sing* **LILI** *into the circle. Finally,* **LILI** *smiles despite herself – look at these two weirdos singing. It's a little fun.* **LILI** *stands up and starts to dance.* **NAN** *hoots.)*

JOEY.   I HATE THIS

(All three **WOMEN** *dance, jumping around the place. Maybe* **JENNIFER** *grabs* **JOEY** *and spins him around playfully in the dance [though he hates it].)*

I HATE THIS

(As **JENNIFER** *dances with him, he plays dead. The song plays. The mood is joyous and free, like a fun girls sleepover until –)*

(Suddenly, the phone rings and the **WOMEN** *all stop immediately, panting.* **JENNIFER** *looks odd. Like maybe she's gonna be sick. She runs into the bathroom.* **NAN**, *keys jangling, races over. The song still plays...)*

(Note! Don't get too hung up on the details I just wrote out. The point is, **LILI***'s SAT comment casts a pall over the room and* **NAN** *in her sweet way gets everyone to dance together [sloppy improv, not choreographed], and it's a fun party where we finally see* **JENNIFER** *let loose for the first time – we see a glimpse of her personality. Until the phone interrupts it.)*

NAN. *(Answering.)* Hello! You've reached your home for donuts on Cranberry Highway –

CHUCK. What now?

> *(She looks at **LILI**. Like, "just my idiot husband.")*

JOEY. IS IT OVER

I HATE SONGS

LILI. Yeah.

NAN. Oh, Chuck –

JOEY. THAT WAS ABUSE

NAN. *(To **JOEY**, even though still on the phone.)* You're fine –

JOEY. *(Fake crying.)* No I'm not. I'm not.

NAN. *(On the phone.)* Well…

Did you try the red AND the blue?

What about the Citibank – the little one with the silver –

None?

Hm.

> *(She turns her back slightly to everyone. This is perhaps the first time she speaks in a normal volume. So for her, it's quiet.)*

Don't you have any cash?

You KNOW it doesn't drop in 'til tomorrow morning.

Five a.m. is morning, not night DO NOT SPLIT HAIRS

Well, I wasn't tracking –

Do *not* blame me for that, Christmas Tree Shops has wonderful spices.

I put that on the Job Lot card anyway!

And I'm not the one who charged $9.95 plus tax and tip for a Buffalo Chicken Wrap at the 99 last week, pal.

Well, how much over?

*(Pause. **JENNIFER** comes out of the bathroom.)*

NAN. WELL TAKE IT OUT OF THE BAHAMA FUND.

You're what?

Well, then tell him you'll be right back and THEN take it out of the Bahama Fund.

I mean, it's only twelve dollars.

Just do it. I give up. We'll pay the overdraft –

YES. YES.

No, I won't *guilt you later Chuck.*

When have I *guilted you later*????

(Pause.)

Well.

That was DIFFERENT.

(Pause.)

Well, you can replenish it tomorrow after the direct deposit –

Okay.

Yes.

Yes.

HI BRANDON

I LOVE YOU

Tell him I love him

WHO'S A GOOD BOY BRANDON

WHO'S MOMMY'S BEST BOY????

Did you feed him?

CHUCK, IT IS ALMOST ELEVEN P.M.

HE EATS AT EIGHT.

Well!

That's not a funny joke.

No! It's not.

Brandon's health is not a joke to –

FOUR CHUCK.

IT IS ALWAYS FOUR.

Set an ALARM in case you fall asleep. You know I hate –

Then use the one on my side of the bed.

Yes.

Yes.

Turn the volume up to max, for if you roll onto your hearing ear –

I SAID TURN THE VOLUME UP.

TURN THE VOLUME U–

(Pause. She's maybe a little quiet again.)

It's fine.

I promise.

I won't guilt you later, it's not your –

Yes, I mean it.

YES CHUCK.

YES.

When I say YES I mean YES. God.

Yes.

Okay.

Okay.

NAN. I love you too.

(*Flirtatious.*) Oh Chuck.

Chuck! I'm at work.

(*She looks over at* **LILI** *and* **JENNIFER**, *who politely look away.* **JOEY** *stares.* **NAN** *makes a face at him.*)

(*He hisses at her.*)

(**JENNIFER** *shushes him.*)

Drive safely the roads are –

Yes, twelve dollars is fine.

I promise.

Oh! I'm getting a beep!

CHUCK

I HAVE TO GO IT COULD BE THE TOW TRUCK

(**JENNIFER** *looks over.*)

No! Not for me.

THOUGH THAT DAMN THING IS STILL RATTLING –

It's for a customer –

CHUCK I HAVE TO GO

Bye.

Bye.

Yes!

Bye.

I SAID YES GOODBYE CHUCK.

*(She pushes the other line. In a completely
different voice, a courteous one:)*

Hello! You've reached your home for Donuts on
Cranberry Highway.

Oh! Hi, Ed.

*(**LILI**'s gaze darts over.)*

Yes, of course.

Oh no, she's a doll *here*. The boys were just like that, so
I know.

Haha!

Oh yes, of course.

I think you should come get her YES!

She's only on a short shift...

And she told me about the test.

Well, and the weather...of course. You don't want to be
out there much longer.

It's supposed to accumulate all night, so... Ha.

*(She winks at **LILI**.)*

You know she *would have called you, but she didn't
have her phone* and this one was tied up...

*(**LILI** smiles at **NAN**. **LILI** slides off the stool,
goes over to the phone, waiting.)*

Yes, she's right here.

Of course.

Ha.

Of course.

Give Maria a big kiss for me.

NAN. Just lean on down and give her a big kiss.

Alright.

Okay. Alrighty!

Here she is –

> *(She hands* **LILI** *the phone, she smiles a little.
> As* **LILI** *talks, she goes over and starts rotating
> and flipping donuts on the trays.)*

LILI. Hi *Dad.*

I told you! The weather is...

No, I called from here.

Despite that being very inconvenient.

I'm ready.

Yes.

Fiiiiine.

I will.

I said I will! I meant I WILL.

Kloveyou2bye.

> *(She hangs up.)*

My dad said to say thanks for letting me off early, which
obviously I would have said. He thinks I'm a CHILD.

But, thank you. For real, Nan. You're the best.

NAN. Well, I wouldn't want you to bomb the test because
I made you stay and flip donuts.

LILI. *(Totally oblivious.)* Thank god it's only 'til I get into
school in a few months or I'd kill myself.

> **(NAN** *clocks that. But* **LILI** *genuinely doesn't.
> It's not cruel.)*

Can I go in the other room and study until my dad comes?

NAN. *(Don't you dare make this heavy or mean too much.)* Of course, smartie.

> *(**LILI** smiles, she dashes off into the break room. **NAN** keeps flipping. A palpable silence.)*

She's a good kid.

Her mother is a doll.

JOEY. She seems like a brat.

JENNIFER. Joey! Stop.

JOEY. I'm old, I'm allowed to say whatever I want.

JENNIFER. No one's allowed to say whatever they want.

> *(**NAN** flips.)*

JOEY. I'm hungry.

NAN. *(To **JENNIFER**.)* I can make him a Wake-Up Wrap.

JOEY. EXTRA BACON

NAN. Who's a brat now?

> *(**JOEY** grins.)*

JOEY. Me!

> *(**NAN** opens the microwave to make the wrap.)*

JENNIFER. I used to have a Bahama fund too...well, mine was called the Disney fund.

NAN. Oh yeah? You ever make it to Disney?

JENNIFER. We sure did. For our twentieth. On the first night, my husband got sick at a shrimp buffet. He spent the rest of the trip eating Saltines in between vomiting and diarrhea spells.

JOEY. I'M ABOUT TO EAT

JENNIFER. Disney. The happiest place on Earth.

*(**NAN** laughs.)*

NAN. Yeah, I figure I'll never get to the Bahamas. But it doesn't hurt to keep the dream alive. But there's always a new muffler, or a root canal, or a new water heater or or or...you know.

JENNIFER. I sure do.

*(**NAN** picks up the tip jar that's been tucked near the register. It's covered with tiny plastic palm trees and a little plastic flamingo. It says "SEND NAN TO THE BAHAMAS.")*

NAN. Couple of years ago, the younger kids – you know, the college summer kids who work here on break – they decorated the tip jar for me.

JENNIFER. "Send Nan to the Bahamas."

JOEY. TACKY

NAN. *(Urgently!)* I mean we split it! We split it! Of course!

JENNIFER. Okay –

NAN. But I thought it was nice. It's nice. And you never know. Maybe someday someone will leave $2,349.99 in here just for me. That'd get me the cruise package Chuck and I have been eyeing. The one with the build your own pasta bar. Ziti for days!

(The microwave beeps.)

JENNIFER. Sounds safer than a shrimp buffet!

NAN. Oh you bet, you bet!

JOEY. WHERE'S MY FOOD

NAN. Alright, you! Take a chill pill.

JOEY. HUH

(**NAN** *plates the wrap. She rounds the counter.*
JOEY *shoves his in his mouth and begins to
chew.*)

IT'S HOT

JENNIFER. Be careful, Joe.

JOEY. *(Mouth full.)* IT'S TOO LATE

NOW I'M BURNED

JENNIFER. You'll be fine.

JOEY. This is abuse!

(**JENNIFER** *reaches over and grabs the
uneaten part of his wrap.*)

THAT'S MINE

(**JENNIFER** *blows on Joey's wrap to cool it
down. He watches. She hands it back. He
takes a small bite. He's satisfied. He eats
quietly. After a moment, Nan hands Jennifer
her own warmed wrap.*)

JENNIFER. Oh, wow, thanks. You didn't have to.

(**JENNIFER** *takes out her wallet.* **NAN** *shakes
her head.*)

NAN. Your money's no good here.

(**JENNIFER** *is moved, but* **NAN** *doesn't notice.
She just looks around the place.* **JENNIFER**
takes a small bite of her wrap.)

Ugh, everything is always dirty. Nothing is ever clean.

(**JENNIFER** *nods like "Oh I know what you
mean."*)

NAN. I don't think Chuck has ever ever thought about that. He sleeps the *gentle sleep* of a person who *has never cleaned out the fridge or easy off'd the oven.*

JENNIFER. *(Laughing.)* Oh my god BILL WOULD NEVER!

NAN. Do you think our husbands have EVER laid awake wondering if they cleaned out the coffee pot well enough?

JENNIFER. Or if that little grate inside the microwave still has food in it?

NAN. Or how in the hell to get the splatter off the wall behind the stove? WILL IT EVER COME OFF???

JENNIFER. *(Laughing.)* Haha! When I think about all the times I forgot to shampoo my hair because I was worrying about if the trash liners were slipping down in the garbage –

NAN. Or if the linen closet was organized by towels and pillowcases –

JENNIFER. Or color!

(**JENNIFER** *laughs.*)

NAN. It boggles the mind!

JOEY. *(Mouth full.)* You're both lazy.

(**NAN** *goes over and snatches his wrap from him.* **JENNIFER** *laughs.* **NAN** *holds it over his head, teasing.*)

NAN. What did you say? Hm?

JOEY. GIMME MY WRAP

NAN. Take it back...

JOEY. NO

NAN. *(Still dangling the wrap.)* I SAID

Take it back.

JOEY. FINE

NAN. FINE *WHAT?*

JOEY. FINE YOU AREN'T LAZY

> *(She smugly smiles and hands him his wrap back. He shoves it in his mouth so there's none left.)*

(Mouth full.) YOU'RE JUST UGLY!

JENNIFER. Joey!

NAN. Oh, I don't care what he says.

JOEY. WHY? YOU SHOULD CARE WHAT I SAY

JENNIFER. You sound like my father.

NAN. Honestly, men are so sensitive.

JENNIFER. Oh god yes! Last week Bill gave me the silent treatment because I told him the shirt he got at a yardsale – it had like, bears on it – didn't fit –

NAN. OH HO HO!!!! Rookie mistake!

JENNIFER. He wouldn't talk to me for the whole night.

NAN. Bet that was a nice change!

JENNIFER. You know, it really fuckin' was.

They do the same thing if you don't laugh at their jokes –

NAN. Or you're faster at assembling furniture –

JENNIFER. Oh! Or if you accidentally move their Rogaine from the back of the bathroom cabinet!

NAN. Haha! Like we don't notice they use it!

Or how they get mad when you ask them to put the seat down.

JENNIFER. Mad? Oh, they're like weirdly proud of it. Like, "A man peed here!"

NAN. Huh, well that explains Chuck's aim.

JENNIFER. DON'T YOU DARE TRY TO SHOW THEM ANYTHING ABOUT EMAIL OR THE COMPUTER!

NAN. Or explain the plots of movies to them! Brad Pitt and Edward Norton are the same person!

JENNIFER. *"Citizen Kane* is the best movie ever made!" Rosebud was the SLED!

JOEY. No, it was her HOOHA!

JENNIFER. Oh God. It's an emotional ODYSSEY if you make more money than them –

NAN. *(Laughing.)* Or if you tell them you think they said something rude at a barbecue!

JENNIFER. *(Laughing.)* They're so fragile. It's sort of sad!

JOEY. NO WE AREN'T

SHUT UP

SHUT UP

(The **WOMEN** *burst out laughing.)*

NAN. See???

JENNIFER. And OH WOW don't you DARE get mad when they call watching their own kids

JENNIFER & NAN. "babysitting" –

JOEY. WHAT ELSE DO YOU CALL IT

JENNIFER & NAN. HAHAHAHA

JOEY. SHUT UP

SHUT UP

SHUT UP

JENNIFER. It's ALSO HILARIOUS TO ME HOW MANY OF THEM THINK THEY HAVE A RICH INNER LIFE!

HAHAHA

HAHAHA

NAN. I wish I had time for an inner life!

HAHAHAHAHAHA

HAHAHAHA

HAHAHA

JENNIFER. *(In hysterics.)* Oh and we know they don't actually have one!

HAHAHA

NAN. It's true! It's TRUE! One time Chuck started building *SHIPS IN A BOTTLE!*

HAHAHA

JENNIFER. HAHAHAHAHAHA

HAHAHA Ships in a – Bill welds! He welds now! He welds things together! It's all over the yard! He bought a helmet and everything!

HAHAHHA

Oh my god! HAHAHAHA

They're so boring…hahaha they are so DULL

EVERY TIME THEY TALK I WANT TO FALL ASLEEP

Oh! Oh! And this morning Bill stubbed his toe!

And it's like every time he does that, suddenly he's the Hulk – RAAWRR RAWWRH!

(She imitates the Hulk…badly.)

NAN. Oh, Chuck too! One time he bumped his elbow on the door jamb and it was like he was starring in *Saving Private Ryan* –

(She acts like she's been shot. Moaning and crying dramatically while **JENNIFER** *keeps "Hulking." The* **WOMEN** *are beside themselves with laughter now. Tears rolling down their cheeks.)*

NAN. HAHAHA

OH GOD OH GOD

HAHAHAHAHA

HAHAHAHA *AND THEN THERE WAS THE TIME*

Chuck and I kept trying to save our marriage with another kid!

JENNIFER. Hahahahaha

hahaha

HAHAHA OH GOD

BEEN THERE! BEEN THERE!

HAHAHA THAT'S REAL THAT'S REAL HAHAHA

NAN. And now I hate motherhood!

JOEY. I'm scared.

This is scary.

(They burst out laughing. They just die.)

NAN. *(Calming a little.)* But I do like each kid individually. Sometimes. When they're being funny or a human. Or when they're accomplishing something that reflects well on me. Not that my kids EVEN DO THAT HAHAHAHA!

JENNIFER. Mine neither!

Mine neither!

NAN. But I guess that's kind of my fault because I dropped my firstborn. Twice!

(They burst out into hysterics again. **JOEY** *starts to scream.)*

JOEY.	**NAN & JENNIFER.**
AHHHHHHHHHHHHH	HAHAHAHAHAHA HA
AHHHHHHHHHHHHHH	HAHAHA!!!!!
AHHHHHHHHHHHH	HAHAHAHAHAHAHA HA

*(***JOEY*** starts banging the table and screaming. He flips over an adjacent chair. The* **WOMEN** *both look at each other. An idea. They go over to* **JOEY.***)*

(They start to wheel him towards the bathroom.)

JENNIFER. *(To* **JOEY,** *laughing.)* Does Joey need a time out?

NAN. *(Laughing.)* He sure does!

JOEY. WITCHES

BITCHES

WITCHES

BITCHES

I AM AN ADULT

THIS IS ABUSE

(Laughing, they open the bathroom door and gently push him in. They shut the door. **NAN** *finds a key on her large jangling chain.* **JENNIFER** *covers her mouth like, "OH MY GOD! Are we gonna do it?"* **NAN** *nods. The* **WOMEN** *giggle as* **JOEY** *still carries on…* **NAN** *locks the door.* **JOEY** *bangs, the* **WOMEN** *keep giggling, helpless church giggles.)*

JOEY. I'm reporting you to social services!

> (*Both* **WOMEN** *burst out laughing again. They slide down and sit in front of the door as* **JOEY** *keeps banging on it.*)

I NEED MY MEDICINE OR I'LL DIE

> (**JENNIFER** *looks at* **NAN**, *rolling her eyes. She mouths "he doesn't" – they giggle some more.*)

JENNIFER. (*Still giggling.*) Prove it!

JOEY. (*Furiously screaming from inside the bathroom.*) You are. You're both lazy. You're lazy and you won't take me back to the movie.

I wanna go home.

I wanna watch the movie.

I wanna go.

I WANNA WATCH *SINGIN' IN THE RAIN*

I'll never get to see the guy WALK UP A WALL

You're both monsters!

> (*They hear banging in the bathroom. He's breaking something. It's now not so funny.* **JENNIFER** *stands and helps* **NAN** *up. Another bang. Bang bang – what is he breaking?!* **NAN** *fumbles for her keys.*)

JENNIFER. (*Serious now.*) Joey, stop –

> (**JOEY** *is still inside, banging around, maybe we hear porcelain breaking.*)

JOEY. LAZY

LAZY

STUPID

LAZY

LAZY

STUPID

LAZY

LAZY

JENNIFER. (*Getting super pissed.*) JOEY YOU STOP THAT RIGHT NOW

(**NAN** *tries to open the door. She can't.*)

NAN. (*To* **JENNIFER**.) The door! He's holding it.

(**JENNIFER** *gets right up to the door and starts banging it.*)

JENNIFER. LISTEN JOEY THIS IS NOT FUNNY

(**NAN** *tries to budge the lock again.* **JOEY** *starts to laugh.*)

JOEY. WHO IS LAUGHING NOW

HAHAHAH

HAHAHA

YOU STUPID BITCHES

YOU UGLY DUMB BITCHES

(**JENNIFER** *bangs on the door. She really starts to lose it.*)

JENNIFER. (*Screaming, banging, just fucking out of her mind.*) LISTEN HERE YOU

OPEN THIS DOOR

JOEY. (*Sing-songing.*)
JENNY JENNY LIKE A PENNY

JENNIFER. (*Banging.*) Joe, OPEN THIS DOOR. NOW.

JOEY. *(Singing.)*

JENNY JENNY LIKE A

Fuck you I'm in charge now hahahahahahahaha

> *(**JENNIFER** starts banging like a truly insane person, **NAN** takes a step back. It's scary.)*

JENNIFER. NO

NO

NO

STOP FUCKING SINGING

YOU ASSHOLE

> *(**JENNIFER** is at the peak of psychosis. She is red-faced and screaming and kicking at the door and finally forces herself in.)*

> *(**JENNIFER** whips open the door of the bathroom and **JOEY** is standing up at the door frame, out of the wheelchair. He's holding the wall to be upright, but the surprise of the door opening makes him stumble into the room a bit. He holds on to the wall as she gets right in his face. Her voice is low, almost menacing.)*

Listen, you disgusting, pathetic old fuck.

I've been cleaning up your SHIT and your PISS

FOR THREE YEARS

YOU WILL

SHUT THE FUCK UP

YOU WILL

You owe me

YOU OWE ME FOR TAKING CARE OF YOU

I never complained

I never ONCE complained about how you've treated me –

Which is like your personal servant

You never think of me for ONE SECOND when I leave your room

You could give a fuck less about me

But here's the great news.

I don't give a fuck about you either.

I'm done!

I'm done!

I'm fucking done forever

YOU CAN'T MAKE ME DO IT ANYMORE

…

I should just

I should just LEAVE YOU HERE

I SHOULD LEAVE YOU HERE AND MAKE YOU SIT IN YOUR SHIT

SIT IN YOUR OWN SHIT FOR AWHILE

SIT IN YOUR OWN SHIT FOR AS LONG AS

I

TELL

YOU.

>　(**JOEY** *smiles. A slow grin. He screws up his face. He grunts quietly. He's pushing. He looks right into* **JENNIFER**'s *eyes.)*

Don't you dare.

(**JOEY** *is still smiling. His face is beet red. He pushes. He maintains eye contact with* **JENNIFER**. *A standoff.*)

JENNIFER. I SAID DON'T YOU DARE

NAN. …is he?

JENNIFER. JOEY.

NO.

JOEY. *(While still pushing.)* HAHAHAHA

HAHAHAHAHA

EEEEEEE

HAHAHAHAHAHAHA

JENNIFER. *(Kicking his wheelchair a little.)* JOEY DON'T EVEN THINK ABOUT –

(*A horrifying sound. And I want to be clear. This is not a funny fart joke. I personally never find scatological jokes or bits funny. This is not that. This is the menacing sound of an old, sexist prick who just purposefully shit his pants. He shit his pants to show this woman what power he has.*)

(*Perhaps we don't need a sound. Perhaps he's just done. And he sits. Daring her to murder him. He is willing to soil himself just to make her feel small. A sinister grin spreads across his face.*)

(*There's a deadly silence.* **JENNIFER** *looks like she's going to burst into flames or pull off her skin or bash her head against the wall or pass out or laugh. She does none of those things. She just. She just sits.*)

NAN. *(To* **JOEY**, *who is – pardon the pun – wearing a shit-eating grin.)* You're a horrible person.

JOEY. *(A slow, smug smile then...menacingly.)* ...Prove it.

NAN. *(To* **JENNIFER,** *who is now almost catatonic, sitting on the floor.)* Jennifer, why don't you get some air and –

JENNIFER. *(To* **JOEY?** *To her husband? To the universe?)* This is how you ALL ARE

THIS IS HOW YOU ALL ARE

You never think about anything but what YOU want to do

ALL OF *YOU*

You get to sit in your room with your crossword puzzles and FUCK WITH ME

AND

My whole life –

I would die for just one minute

I've been married for seven thousand, six hundred and sixty-five days and I know that not ONE of those days has my husband made dinner

NOT ONE

NOT ONE SINGLE ONE

NEVER EVER NEVER

He never did

And once when I had walking pneumonia, he offered to take the kids to the GROUND ROUND and then he took the cash out of my wallet to do it

And he wanted me to THANK HIM –

NAN. *(Approaching to comfort, trying to sit with her.)* Jennifer –

JENNIFER. *(Shrinking away, focusing on* **NAN,** *coming back to herself.)* I'm so angry

JENNIFER. I'm so angry

I'm so angry

I'm so angry

I'll die FURIOUS FOREVER AND EVER

It's killing me

PLEASE

HELP

HELP

NAN. Hon…

JENNIFER. *I'm sorry*

I'm sorry

I'm sorry

I just

I can't I can't I can't

NAN. It's okay, calm down.

Take a breath.

> *(She holds her for a second, there on the floor.*
> *Rocking her. Taking care of her.)*

You're okay. You're okay.

JENNIFER. I'm not

I'm not okay

I'm not

NAN. I'm here, it's –

JENNIFER. *(Starting to scream, she's afraid of what she'll do to him.)* GET HIM OUT OF HERE

I CAN'T LOOK AT HIM GET HIM OUT OF HERE

GET HIM AWAY

GET HIM AWAY

GET HIM OUT

> (**NAN** *sort of panic-wheels him to the bathroom, helping him back into his chair.*)

JOEY. She has to change me!

SHE HAS TO CHANGE ME

CHANGE ME

CHANGE ME

IT'S YOUR JOB

NAN. Hush, Joey!

> (**NAN** *puts him in the bathroom and he starts to get a little more nervous.*)

> (**NAN** *closes him in, locking it, not violently and not with menace, but so she can have a second to tend to* **JENNIFER** *and so he can be safe in case* **JENNIFER** *loses it. From inside the bathroom we hear:*)

JOEY. *YOU CAN'T GET OUT OF IT*

IT'S YOUR JOB

YOUR ONLY JOB

> (**NAN** *doesn't know what to say. Maybe for the first time in her whole life.*)

> (**JOEY** *starts to bang on the door relentlessly. The* **WOMEN** *say nothing.* **NAN** *just watches* **JENNIFER**, *who is curled up in a ball on the floor.*)

(He bangs some more. He screams "ahhhhhhhh" sometimes while banging. It shifts. He's obviously knocking his head on the door.)

*(**JOEY** continues "I'm the boss" knocking throughout the following section. After a moment or two of this, **NAN** goes to **JENNIFER**. She gets down on the ground with her [not easy for a senior citizen such as herself] She's about to put her arm around **JENNIFER** when –)*

JENNIFER. *(Soberly.)* There's no tow truck coming.

NAN. What?

JENNIFER. There's no tow truck. I never called one. There's NO TOW TRUCK.

JOEY. I'M THE BOSS *(Knock.)*

I'M THE BOSS *(Knock.)*

NAN. Jennifer –

JENNIFER. I think. I think I'm leaving. I was leaving.

NAN. Leaving?

JENNIFER. I don't know...

JOEY. I'M THE BOSS *(Knock.)*

I'M THE BOSS *(Knock.)*

NAN. Jennifer, do I need to call someone...your husband –

JENNIFER. *(Suddenly.)* No! Please! No!

NAN. Jennifer...you're scaring me –

JOEY. *(Enraged, screaming.)* YOU COME FIX THIS

FIX ME NOW

THAT'S YOUR JOB

JENNIFER. *(Reciting, almost to herself at first.)* I picked him up.

I wheeled him to the van.

I buckled him in and I pulled out of his doctor's parking lot and I just –

I didn't stop.

Exit 23

Exit 24

Exit 25 – that's ours – I always think every time I take it

I think what if I didn't

Like when you stand on a high stairway or bleachers or a sea ledge

What if you just jumped

I mean, you don't jump

You don't really want to

But part of you thinks *what if I did*

What if I passed the exit

What if keep going

Where would I be

Where would I end up

Suddenly I thought if I just drove and drove and drove

Somehow I would finally, blissfully end up alone

I would end up in peace at the edge of the world, or something...

I say it now and it sounds –

　　　(She starts to get a little emotional maybe?)

JOEY. I'M THE BOSS

I'M THE BOSS

JENNIFER. I sound crazy.

I feel crazy.

I'm sorry

I'm sorry

But I can't go back, I can never go back

I know it, I'll just –

Please, Nan. Please.

You have to help me.

I think if I could just go, if I could leave it all behind, I could listen to myself.

I could be okay.

JOEY. I'M THE BOSS *(Knock.)*

I'M THE BOSS *(Knock.)*

I'M THE BOSS *(Knock.)*

JENNIFER. I know you know what I mean!

I know you do!

NAN. *(Almost relieved, she gets this.)* Jennifer, Jennifer… of course I do. When my kids – well most of 'em – left the house, I felt the same way. What was I? What had I done? But it's okay…you'll find yourself again. You'll figure it out –

JENNIFER. I'm forty-five years old.

Find myself again?

It's too late. I already did it all wrong.

I look over at Bill on his chair watching the game and I *want him dead.*

JOEY. I'M THE BOSS *(Knock.)*

I'M THE BOSS *(Knock. Knock. Knock.)*

NAN. Jennifer, *everyone* wants their husband dead! We all go to our graves resenting them. That's normal! Heck, I shot Chuck with a BB gun once...maybe even twice! Just a sort of SCIENCE experiment...to see him GET UP OFF HIS RECLINER. That's normal –

JOEY. I'M THE BOSS *(Knock.)*

NAN. And that's what makes us strong...what makes us better than them is *we keep going. We are women.* We just said it! Men are sensitive. We are tough. That's the world.

JENNIFER. But WHY? It doesn't have to be this way.

JOEY. I'M THE BOSS *(Knock.)*

(Knock)

(Knock)

(Knock)

(A small pause. Has he tired himself out? For now.)

NAN. All we can do is do our best. Take care of the kids. Get a laugh or two in. Sometimes there's a girls trip to the Casino. A cookout. No one's life is a picnic. Even Princess Diana died in a car wreck!

(A silence.)

JENNIFER. *(Gesturing to the bathroom door.)* Let me leave him here.

*(**NAN** gives a look like "Oh fuck no.")*

Please. Give me some time to get away and then...

I'll give you the number of the home, you can call them...you can...return him?

NAN. Jesus, Jennifer, he's not a LIBRARY BOOK.

JENNIFER. I know, I know, but –

NAN. I can't get involved. I feel for you, I do, your forties
        are hard, but –

JENNIFER. Nan –

NAN. Get back in the van. Go back to the home. Tell them
        you got lost.

JENNIFER. I didn't get lost.

I'm not lost.

NAN. You'll get arrested for…kidnapping! Or elder abuse,
        or – what about your girls?

JENNIFER. They wouldn't even notice I was gone.

NAN. Wait…

I –

This is not my problem.

And

And

And

This has gone too far, I have to call –

(*She heads towards the phone and picks it up.*
JENNIFER *races to try and stop her.*)

JENNIFER. (*Truly looking her in the eye.*) Nan, please,
        I know you understand!

Don't call, just listen to me. Please.

Staying here is killing me.

Help me.

(*Suddenly, headlights come from the window
– someone is arriving. Then, a loud honking
from outside.*)

NAN. *(Shouting into the break room.)* Lili?

> *(**LILI** comes whipping out of the break room, holding her SAT prep books. **NAN** puts the phone down quickly, **JENNIFER** dries her tears and runs back from behind the counter to the table, **NAN** grabs a rag making like she's been wiping down the milk containers.)*

LILI. *(Screaming, oblivious to the tension.)* BE RIGHT THERE *DAD*

> *(She turns to **NAN**.)*

LILI. Hey Nan, thanks for letting me study.

NAN. *(Trying to seem casual.)* Of course, sweetheart.

LILI. I promise to do extra side work on my next shift. I'm in Monday night.

NAN. Tell your dad next time, he should let you call in. He should know school is the most important thing. You gotta ace that test.

LILI. *(Casual, on a laugh.)* Yeah! Otherwise I could be working *HERE* the rest of my life! What a NIGHTMARE!

> *(**NAN** hears that. **LILI** notices. Tiny beat. Do not make it too big or dramatic.)*

I mean for me. It's a great job and everything, obviously.

NAN. *(A laugh.)* Of course, but no one expects you to work here forever. You've got big California dreams, kid!

LILI. *(Relieved **NAN** doesn't seem mad, she rolls her eyes.)* Ohio, Nan! Oberlin is in Ohio!

NAN. *(Joking.)* That's right, the big city.

> *(A second of silence. **NAN** pastes on a smile.)*

Hey. Lemme give you a good luck squeeze for tomorrow.

(**LILI** *obliges, putting her books down, she goes to* **NAN** *and they embrace.* **JENNIFER** *still in the corner, sort of hiding a little. Trying to stay out of the way.*)

LILI. Thanks again, Nan. See you Monday.

(**LILI** *is gone.* **NAN** *looks after her a long moment. Quiet. She tosses her rag from one hand to the other back to the other. She looks at the phone. She turns to* **JENNIFER.**)

NAN. Leave.

JENNIFER. What?

NAN. You're leaving. Get out. Now.

JENNIFER. Are you –

NAN. I'll give you thirty minutes of lead time. Then I HAVE to call the cops.

We should trade cars – the logo on the van –

(**NAN** *fiddles with her lanyard. She takes off some of the keys.*)

My car's the Oldsmobile. It's missing the passenger side mirror, so be careful.

JENNIFER. Nan, no, I can't take your car –

NAN. You can abandon it somewhere, they'll get it back to me. Call in an anonymous tip from a payphone and then take off.

JENNIFER. I've already asked too much, Nan...that's too much.

NAN. (*Handing her the keys.*) I'll get him home.

JENNIFER. (*Refusing the keys.*) Nan, no –

(**NAN** *takes her by the shoulders. Looks her dead in the eyes.*)

NAN. Jennifer.

Don't take care of me.

I'm fine.

And you still have time.

I'm saying you can go.

Be free.

> (**JOEY** *cries out from the bathroom. He probably just woke up after his little tantrum. He's of course still covered in shit.*)

JOEY. *(Sincere.)* Is anyone there?

> (**JENNIFER** *and* **NAN** *look to the bathroom door.*)

Help Help

I'm sorry, I'll be good, I promise.

It smells bad –

NAN. *(Calling out.)* Coming, Joe.

> (**JENNIFER** *doesn't move.*)

(Getting a little angry.) This is what you wanted. I'm giving it to you.

> (*She holds the car keys. After a second or two,* **JENNIFER** *finally reaches for them.* **NAN** *quickly packs a bunch of donuts in a box and hands it to* **JENNIFER**.)

I guess take these guys, too. Best not to stop for anything for a long ways.

> (**NAN** *picks up the Bahama Fund jar. She absolutely unsentimentally empties it, folds the bills and pours the change in her hands. She holds it all out to* **JENNIFER**.)

(Maybe tears fall down **JENNIFER**'s *face. Maybe not.)*

NAN. …Make sure you pump the brakes if you hit a patch of ice.

(That is how women of a certain age in New England say "I am with you. I hear you. You are seen." But they're a bit too crusty, too hardened, too worn to say it. **JENNIFER** *reaches forward. Not for the money. For* **NAN**. *She hugs her for a long time. She finally lets go.)*

JENNIFER. Thank you.

*(***NAN*** thrusts the money in* **JENNIFER**'s *hand.)*

NAN. *(Moving away.)* You'd better go.

Thirty minutes.

I'm serious.

*(***JENNIFER*** gathers her coat, stuffs the money in her pockets and races out. The doorbell jangles.* **NAN** *stares. For a long while. She puts the jar back. She rights Jennifer's chair. She looks at the clock.)*

JOEY. Jenny?

Please?

(Slowly, she grabs a huge roll of toilet paper from under the counter and the bag **JENNIFER** *left where she was sitting.)*

(She goes into the bathroom. Presumably to change **JOEY**. *Then.)*

(The lights shift. The **ACTRESS WHO PLAYS LILI** *steps onstage, outside the frame of the*

donut store. Perhaps on the apron, or an entrance vom or something. She speaks – it's not smug or mean. Just explaining something. Like a calm TEDTalk, but warmer. She's soothing us. Telling us something casual and pleasing that then escalates in pace and tempo by the end:)

THE ACTRESS WHO PLAYS LILI. Hi everyone. While we wait, I'll be telling you a story about a woman whose husband was her best friend. They were really cute together. They met in law school. She was third in her class, and he was fourth. But I assure you, they were neck and neck. Their wedding, which happened the summer before their last year of school, was featured in the Boston Globe, which sort of embarrassed her and sort of delighted her in equal measure.

They both passed the bar the first time. They both got great jobs clerking for judges. They got a nice apartment – really nice, you could see the Charles – and they bought a lot of IKEA furniture, knowing that someday they would upgrade. They definitely didn't want to have children until they were established. So, they waited. They worked long hours, every day. But honestly? They still found time to do the Sunday crossword for an hour and go to a farmer's market now and then. They were happy.

During this period, this is how a typical day in her week broke down:

Five a.m. wake up, run on the treadmill for a few minutes (Sunday is a rest day), five thirty a.m., shower, get dressed, six a.m., prep two protein smoothies (frozen berries are best for texture) and take some meat out to thaw for dinner, brew the coffee, scrub out their tumblers from the day before so the coffee can go back in, see what's missing from the fridge and make a note to grab it on the way home, sweep the kitchen floor, leave a note for the handyman about the missing shelf in the den, order his mother's birthday present on Amazon (gift wrapped of course). She wanted to shop small, but then it wouldn't have arrived in time.

She might hear her husband wake up and head to the bathroom to get ready. He scrolls on his phone and goes to the bathroom with the shower running before he hops in, singing a little while she pops in to brush her teeth and they chat some, perhaps.

Once he's out and in the bedroom getting dressed and listening to the *Daily* on his Alexa, she puts on her makeup, dries her hair, drinks a bit of the smoothie, puts away the plastic tub with the extension cords he got out last night and left in the center of the room, packs her computer, her purse, extra lipstick as he comments on a bit of tech news. He thinks self-driving cars are dangerous. He picks out a pocket square as she waters the plants, feeds the cat, packs their lunches (The salad dressing is in a separate container so the lettuce won't get soggy) and she grabs them both umbrellas because it might rain. After much deliberation, he has chosen a light purple polka-dotted square, so he heads into the kitchen grabs his protein smoothie. He takes a sip and smiles. "It tastes delicious!" he says. He's always so appreciative. They get in the car, and he drives, dropping her at her office as he goes to his own. They kiss goodbye in the parking lot. They both work for about twelve hours – 'til around eight p.m. She successfully avoids a male coworker in the breakroom – there's been some weirdness since he got a little tipsy at the Christmas party and hit on her...it's fine now, but less of a minefield if she just avoids him unless they're at a meeting or working on something, she scores big points with her female boss who sometimes sees her as competition, but luckily today, seems to be supportive, and between meetings, she listens to several guilt-ridden voicemails from her mother telling her she doesn't call enough. She deletes them and remembers that she has to reschedule therapy on Friday because it's her sister-in-law's bachelorette party. (The theme is eighties pop divas, should she go more "Straight Up" or "Like A Virgin"?) On her way to staff meeting, she overhears one of her male coworkers on the phone with his wife. When he hangs up, he laments to his office mate – another man – that *he* can't just stay home with the baby.

At lunch, she is asked to mentor a new hire while her male co-worker is not asked to do the same thing, but to be fair, the last intern he trained was a nightmare. Took shitty notes. Her husband goes to a lunch at the club with partners (He eats her salad around five p.m. as second lunch in case you're wondering – lettuce still crispy!) Around seven thirty when they're both wrapping up – she has three cases she's second chair on, he's chairing one case, a huge one – he texts her "what's up for dinner?" She sends back an "I'm not sure" and he texts back "sushi emoji question mark." She agrees. He can totally tell she doesn't want to cook. He even orders. He even pays on his card that draws from their joint account. I bet he got the extra salmon sashimi she likes. This is why at their wedding planning meeting she told the planner he was the details man. He is very good with details.

He finally picks her up, and it is raining (thank God for the umbrellas.) He pulls up to the sushi place and she dashes in to grab it and it's all ready. She hops back in the car, calls her mom and leaves her a voicemail back, adds some things to the grocery list she has in her notes app (Should she get the car detailed?) and they go home to have dinner.

He puts the bag on the table and turns on the TV. "Phew! Finally," he says, looking around the room. "It looks great in here!" She smiles. Score! She forgot she remembered to program the Roomba. She gets plates, chopsticks (they prefer their own), tiny soy sauce containers, a bowl for the spicy mussel soup he orders and some napkins. She unpacks and plates it – what a relief not to cook – they eat and watch *White Lotus.*[*] He likes season one better; season two is too slow. When they're done, he whips out his phone to answer some important emails from his assistant and she packs up all the sushi trash – she dumps out the soy sauce in the sink first, it's so gross when it leaks from the trash – and wipes down the table using the special polish to make the finish last longer.

He is still on the phone, typing and texting as she gets in her pjs, brushes her teeth, puts cream on her face – ugh those eye bags! – and gets in bed with her book. She sets an alarm for five a.m., with a label that says what her first meeting is. It helps her with anxiety to immediately wake up and know the first thing that happens to her in the morning. She starts to drift off while reading when her husband climbs into bed next to her. He pulls her close, puts her book down and they spoon like that for a moment in silence. He breathes her in and says, "You smell so good. I love you." She smiles. She's so lucky to have him as a best friend. Looks like they're ready.

> *(She goes to exit. She turns back to the audience and says completely without menace:)*

Have a nice night.

> *(The lights shift back to the donut shop. **NAN** comes back in wheeling **JOEY**. He's wearing new pants. **NAN** is also holding a plastic bag with his soiled pants.)*

JOEY. *(Calling out into the room, softly.)* Jenny?

Hello?

---

[*] If this reference is now dated, feel free to update this to a current "couples show" that a relatively financially-comfortable couple might watch together on a premium network. Bonus points if it's something a man might have opinions on that a woman might naturally disagree with, subtly.

HELLO

I'm sorry!

I said I was sorry!

Please! Come out!

...

NAN. *(Changing the subject.)* You want a donut?

(*A beat. He looks suspicious.*)

JOEY. *(Sullen.)* Yeah.

(**NAN** *parks him for a second. She crosses around and gets him a donut.*)

(*Cautiously calling out.*) Where's Jenny?

NAN. She's gone away for a bit.

JOEY. *(Mouth full.)* How long? I need my medicine.

NAN. *(Crossing with donut.)* You don't take medicine.

JOEY. Prove –

(**NAN** *looks at him. He stops himself. But he still sulks.* **NAN** *hands him the donut. He takes a bite. She goes to the window and looks out.* **JENNIFER** *is gone. She holds there for a second. She looks at the clock.*)

THIS TASTES LIKE SHIT

(**NAN** *ignores him.*)

HEY. I'm talking!

(**NAN** *ignores him.*)

(*She looks out the window where Jennifer's tire tracks are visible to her.*)

JOEY. I SAID I AM TALKING

> (**NAN** *keeps looking. The phone rings.* **NAN** *reluctantly peels herself away from the window to go answer it.*)

Hey.

Are you gonna get that?

> (*It rings again.*)

It's your husband again.

> (*It rings again.*)

GET IT

GET THE PHONE DUMMY

> (*She looks over at* **JOEY** *with the donut he's disgustingly eating. She looks at the door* **JENNIFER** *just walked through. She stops. Looking at the phone.*)

(*Imitating her answering.*) YOUR HOME FOR DONUTS BLAH BLAH BLAH

BLAH BLAH BLAH BLAH

> (*She picks the phone up and hangs it up in a single motion. The phone stops ringing. She's a little surprised at herself.*)

Hey! Hey!

What are you doing?

THAT COULD HAVE BEEN IMPORTANT DUMMY

> (**NAN** *walks away from the phone slowly. She comes around and sits down at a table. It's almost foreign. To sit. To rest.*)

CRAZY LAZY

CRAZY LAZY

CRAZY LAZY

CRAZY LAZY

HEY WHAT ARE YOU DOING?

WHAT ARE YOU DOING?

> (**NAN** *leans back.*)

GET UP

I HATE THIS

GET UP

I HATE THIS

> (**NAN** *shuts her eyes. Relaxes for a moment.*
> *She smiles to herself, just a tiny bit.*)

I HATE THIS

> (*The phone rings again. This time?* **NAN**
> *doesn't look up.*)

End of Play

www.ingramcontent.com/pod-product-compliance
Lightning Source LLC
Chambersburg PA
CDIIW071929130720
47909CB00014B/2825